FOR OPENERS

People use alcohol and other drugs
to celebrate, to escape, to relax, to ease pain.
Sometimes alcohol and drugs
can take on a life of their own.
And where they might have been used
to have fun or ease some pain,
they're now the cause
of more intense pain.

This pain has moved writers to
tell stories of what these substances
can do to our lives,
how they can control us, dominate us.

STORY SUMMARY

SONNY'S BLUES BY JAMES BALDWIN

The story begins in Harlem in in the 1970s, and it's about a man and his younger brother, Sonny. The man discovers that Sonny, a musician, is sent to jail and rehabilitation for peddling and using drugs. Knowing how hard it is to fully recover from drug use, the man has little hope that Sonny will ever kick the habit.

Then the story flashes back to a scene where the man sits in their family home with his mama after his daddy's funeral. She tells her oldest son a story he's never heard before about how his daddy's younger brother died. Now, the man had never known that his father even had a brother but, on this day of his father's funeral, his mother not only told him of his uncle's existence, but she also explained that he was killed suddenly in a car accident by drunk drivers. As the man promises his mama that he will care for his own brother, Sonny, we begin to worry that Sonny, who is impetuous and musical like their father's brother, will meet a similar end.

The man's own life is complicated by his baby daughter's death from polio. But eventually the man writes to Sonny in rehabilitation and assures Sonny that he can come live with him. Sonny is so grateful for his brother's letter that he promises never to go back on drugs—even when he goes back to his music. Though he knows that his brother disapproves of playing jazz for a living, Sonny makes it clear that—no matter what—Sonny must return to his music.

After rehabilitation, while Sonny is living with his brother and family, Sonny convinces his brother to come to the club in Greenwich Village to hear him play piano. As the man listens to Sonny play the blues, he hears in his music all the suffering Sonny has been through. The man also hears in Sonny's blues the suffering of his mother and father and of all those who died long before them. Sonny's blues even brings the man face to face with his own daughter's death and his own grief. Sonny's music brings his brother hope and light in a dark world.

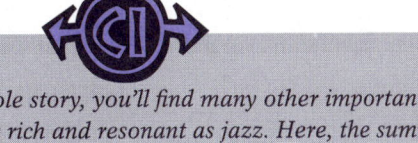

If you can read the whole story, you'll find many other important parts that make the story as rich and resonant as jazz. Here, the summary simply gives a context for the excerpts which follow. Imagine yourself either in the man's or in Sonny's shoes, as you look at and respond to the struggles presented here.

SONNY'S BLUES BY JAMES BALDWIN
STORY EXCERPTS

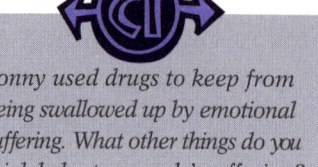

In the flashback, the older brother sits in a dark living room among the "older folk" as he listens to his mama speak. When someone turns on the light, Baldwin writes:

"And when the light fills the room, the child is filled with darkness... The darkness outside is what the old folks have been talking about. It's what they've come from. It's what they endure. The child knows that they won't talk any more because if he knows too much about what's happened to them, he'll know too much too soon, about what's going to happen to him."

What is this darkness that adults know about and children fear? What events in life can create a "darkness?"

When Sonny has returned from drug rehabilitation and is living with his brother, the two men stop one day to listen to a street musician.

Sonny says:

"When she was singing, her voice reminded me for a minute of what heroin feels like sometimes—when it's in your veins. It makes you feel sort of warm and cool at the same time. And distant. And—and sure. It makes you feel in control...

"Listening to that woman sing, it struck me all of a sudden how much suffering she must have had to go through—to sing like that. It's repulsive to think you have to suffer that much."

Sonny used drugs to keep from being swallowed up by emotional suffering. What other things do you think help stop people's suffering?

_____

_____

_____

_____

_____

When Sonny brings his brother to the club, the music of the bass fiddler, Creole, coaxes Sonny to bring out the deepest and best that he has to offer. At one moment, Creole plays and then waits on his fiddle for Sonny "to leave the shoreline and strike out for deep water."

Of that leap, Baldwin writes: "He was Sonny's witness that deep water and drowning were not the same thing—he had been there and he knew... He was waiting for Sonny to do the things on the keys which would let Creole know that Sonny was in the water."

At the end of the story, Baldwin shifts the focus to Creole's music. He tells his audience that his only purpose is to play the blues so that his audience will listen.

"For while the tale of how we suffer, and how we are delighted, and how we may triumph is never new, it always must be heard. There isn't any other tale to tell, it's the only light we've got in all this darkness."

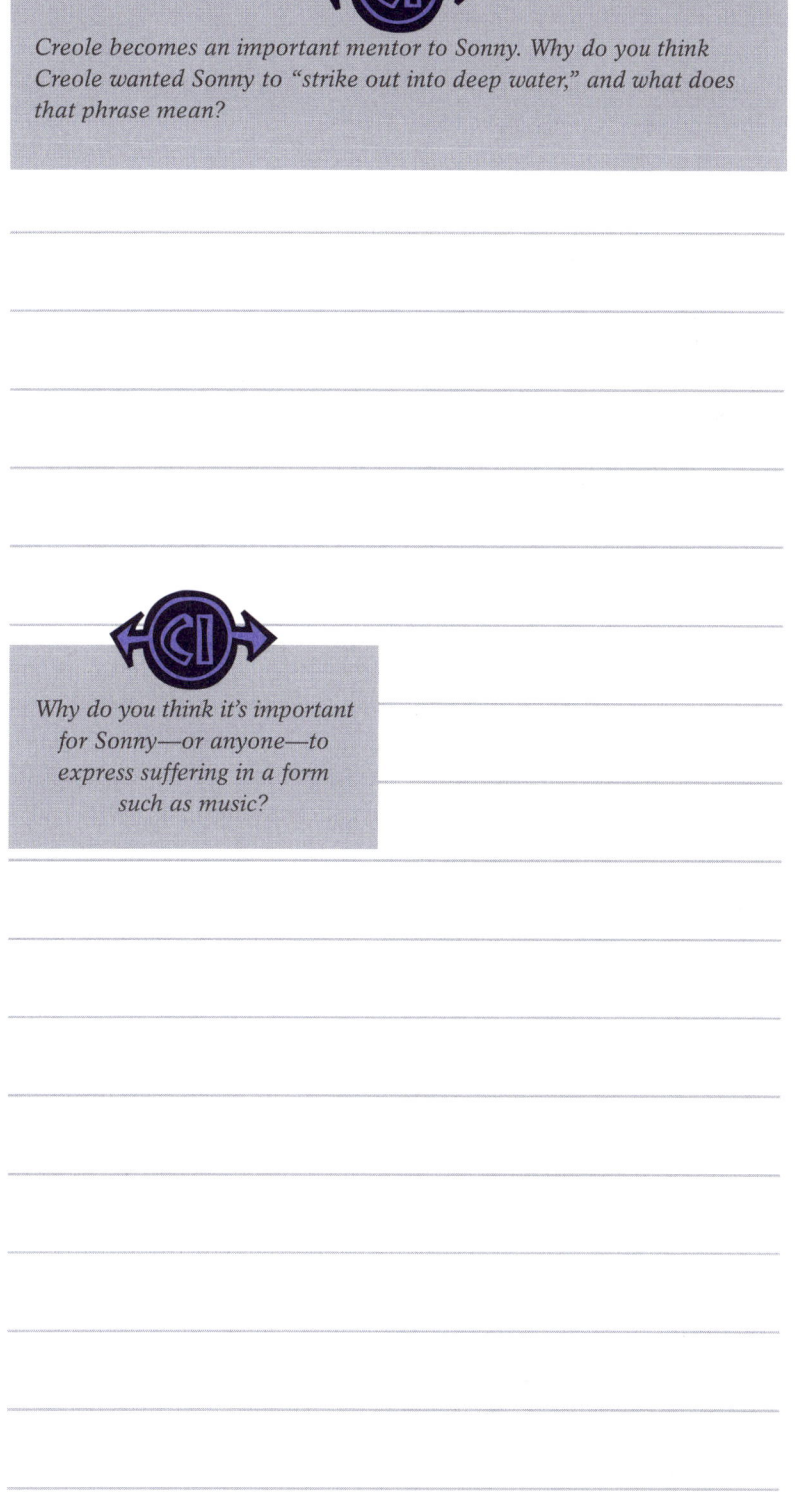

Creole becomes an important mentor to Sonny. Why do you think Creole wanted Sonny to "strike out into deep water," and what does that phrase mean?

Why do you think it's important for Sonny—or anyone—to express suffering in a form such as music?

ALCOHOL
IT STARTED A LONG TIME AGO

Here's a quick look at many ways people have used alcohol through the centuries and at some of the events that affect us.

People have used alcohol in every kind of celebration and tragedy. It is pervasive and accepted.
At the same time, alcohol kills people on highways, destroys self-worth, and impairs family relationships.

What is it about alcohol that makes it such a two-edged sword? Answer here or in a notebook. Then discuss this two-sided nature of alcohol after reading through the historical vignettes.

Early Babylonians and Egyptians found that covering crushed grapes and warmed grains with yeast resulted in a new drink.

Al-kohl is Arabic for finely ground antimony, which means any exotic essence.

Ancient beer was considered to be nutritious food throughout Mesopotamia and Egypt. People said it tasted better than gruel.

The name of the mythological god of wine, Bacchus, is the source for various descriptions of drunkenness. Discuss why you think situations of drunk behavior are often told in humor?

Bacchus, the Roman god of wine (the Greeks called him Dionysus), was always shown holding a bunch of grapes.

About 450 B.C.E. (before the common era), Euripides wrote one of his most famous tragedies, "The Bacchae," a play that deals in part with intoxication for religious reasons.

Have you noticed even the Bible mentions wine and drinking? Why do you think something as controversial as drinking wine could be mentioned in the Bible? Here are some examples:

• In the Book of Exodus, Moses warned his people against excessive drinking.
• In Psalm 4: "Yahweh, you have given more joy to my heart than others ever know, for all their corn and wine."
• In Psalm 104: "Wine makes glad the heart."

• In Psalm 60: "You have allowed your people to suffer, to drink a wine that makes us reel."
• Jesus of Nazareth miraculously transformed water into wine and used wine as the symbol for his blood at the Last Supper.

Bacchanalia began as religious ceremonies and became festivals in Rome and Greece. They degenerated into drunkenness and debauchery, so that today the term "bacchanalian" applies to the same behavior.

"Tannhaeuser," an opera by Wagner, begins with a train of dancers, called bacchantes, who dart wildly among couples lounging on the grass and entice them into a frenzied "Bacchanale."

Medical schools in the Middle Ages distilled alcohol by condensing the vapors into a concentrated drug. A Spanish scholar gave it the name "aqua vitae," the water of life.

The aging process, refined by the monks of the Middle Ages, made wine taste less vinegary.

FRIENDS
A SHORT STORY BY JIM BITNEY

Journal Entry: Day 1

The only reason I'm writing this is because they've got this stupid rule: EVERYBODY KEEP YOUR JOURNAL! Like anybody cares.

A summer camp this place ain't. We get up at 6:30! Actually, that's no problem, cuz my roommate's snoring keeps me up most of the night. The food is totally G-R-O-S-S. The treatment center staff are a bunch of Nazis. My counselor looks like Arnold Schwarzenegger in drag and swears she's Robocop.

The place is crawling with these really weird kids—a bunch of boozers and druggies. What did I ever do to deserve this?

Ted's nose was bleeding. He could feel the blood oozing down and over the corner of his mouth. "Next time you give me any crap, you nerd, I'll knock your teeth out," Rat Jenkins warned him. His real name was Pat, but "Rat" was how everyone knew him. He was two years ahead of Ted, who was in seventh grade.

Ted held his hands at his side. No one in his class had come to defend him, and he hadn't even tried to defend himself. Ted felt like crying. Not because of his nose, not because he was hurting, not because he was afraid, but because he hated Wexford Junior High. He'd been there four weeks and no one was his friend.

Rat punched Ted in the shoulder. "Did you hear what I said, fatso?" Rat's friends laughed. "When I tell you to do something, you do it!"

Suddenly, a smaller boy appeared and stood between Ted and his foe. "Knock it off, you jerk. Leave him alone," the boy said. Ted couldn't remember the boy's name, but he recognized him from social studies class.

Rat just smirked. "Shut up, Al, you freak." With that, Rat sent Al sprawling.

It was kind of like slow motion. Ted could see it happening, but he didn't know how it happened. The fingers of Ted's limp right hand flexed into a tight fist, then moved in a broad arc from his side to the point of the older boy's jaw.

A surprised Ted looked down at Rat, now a crumbled heap that lay at his feet.

"You creamed the dude, Ted. Awesome!" It was Al talking and pulling at Ted's arm. "Come on, let's get out of here." Ted nodded and allowed himself to be pulled away.

In what seemed like only a few minutes later, Ted stood at the kitchen sink at Al's house wiping dried blood from his face and jacket. Al bustled around chattering and piling chips, cookies, and other snacks on the kitchen table. Ted moved to a chair at the table and grabbed some chips. Al opened the refrigerator, pulled out two cans of beer, popped the tops, and sat one in front of Ted.

"Go ahead, dude," Al said taking a pull on his beer. "You deserve it. It's Miller Time."

Ted felt confused. He'd never tasted a beer before, and he'd promised his parents that he wouldn't until he was twenty-one. "I don't know, Al."

"Don't worry, the coast is clear," Al said hastily, noticing his new friend's hesitation.

Ted shifted a little uncomfortably.

"I don't feel like having a beer."

"It's just one beer," Al countered. "It's not going to bite. Here, watch me."

"I'll just have one," Ted said, putting his hand out to take the can. "Today did suck and it'll help me chill out." That afternoon, Al had one. Ted said he'd just have one more beer two more times.

"I'll just have one," Ted said

Journal Entry: Day 5

Three hours of group work!

Everyone was on my case, Man am I

beat! These people want some sort of

eyewitness account of your life or

something. Like I can remember every-

thing! They want me to think about

what sort of friends I have and who I

do things with. Why? So they can tell

me I should dump my friends? No way!

I wish Al was here. He was my only friend. Yeah, I know that no one else in school liked him, but they didn't like me either. All I cared about was that Al liked me.

Al was the only person I felt good with. When we were together, I felt cool. I mean I told my parents that I hated Junior High and that everyone there hated me. They told me just to try harder and be polite. Right! School never got any better, so I just quit talking about it. Instead, me and Al started hangin' with some older kids. They knew how to have a GOOD time! And I felt good that they hung with us.

We'd get together and have a few. Maybe just once a week after school and then on the weekends. One day, Judd brought some vodka, and we mixed it with the beer. I got radically sick and hurled all over the place. So I decided to quit drinking. But after about three weeks, I started to feel crappy about school all over again. Plus, I didn't get to see Al that often, except in school. I started remembering how good it felt to be high. I figured, geez, a few beers would be okay.

Anyway, me and Al went over to Doug's house. He was older and he had some marijuana, so we tried it before we drank. It was cool. I was cool. I decided that I wouldn't drink vodka any more. I'd just drink beer and smoke pot. And it worked because I stopped puking.

"My head hurts so bad!" Al moaned as he and Ted walked the last few blocks to school. "I gotta get some heavy duty aspirin or somethin,' man."

"You don't need any aspirin," Ted laughed, "you need a drink."

"Oh, don't even talk about drinkin,' Ted," Al scowled. "I puked about a million times last night. When I woke up this morning, I had another bloody nose. Plus, I think my dad is on to me. I gotta quit this stuff, dude."

"Give me a break," said Ted. "I had twice as much as you last night, and look at me. I'm doin' fine, and I had the breakfast of champions this morning, dude, Wheaties and beer! Besides, aren't you the guy who wanted to hide a whole case in the snow just yesterday?"

"Yeah, yeah, I know," Al shook his head, "but I ain't been havin' a heck of a lot of fun lately. I mean, I think you're cool, Ted, but those other guys we've been hangin' with. Dude, they're startin' to scare me. Maybe we could just lay off the booze and dope, okay? I'm not kiddin.' I'm really messed. Besides, you quit once last fall, remember?"

"Sure, I quit, but then I felt worse off than before. Admit it, man," Ted said draping his arm around Al's shoulder, "me and you are just party animals!"

The two boys rounded the corner, and the slate-gray facade of Wexford Junior High came into view. Al stopped suddenly, dropped his books and began fumbling in his pocket for a handkerchief.

"Oh, dude," Ted said with disgust, "is your nose bleedin' again? You gotta get yourself together, man. You're startin' to be a real bummer."

Journal Entry: Day 8

"No pain. No gain." That's what the little Nazi said this morning when I told her that 6:30 was too early to be jumpin' out of bed. It's like they've got some sort of slogan for everything around here.

So, like you say that you've got some complications in your life. They say, "Keep it simple." If you tell them that you got other problems besides alcohol and other drugs, they say, "First things first." If you say that you don't understand what they're talkin' about in group, they say, "Progress, not perfection." If you say that you don't think you can hang on much longer without a drink or a hit, they say, "Let go and let God." If you tell 'em about how everyone picks on you at school or home, they say, "SO...the bird craps only on you?" At least that one's funny. And if you say that these slogans are dumb and you can't take any more, they even got a slogan for that. They say, "Take what works, leave the rest."

Heck, the only slogan I like around here is "Easy does it." The problem is, I don't think anyone else around here believes in that one. Cuz, so far, anyway, nothin's been easy.

Mr. Mullins, the counselor at the junior high, looked up from the file he'd been reading, leaned back in his easy chair, and spoke to the sullen looking boy sitting across from him. "According to these mid-quarter reports, Ted," Mr. Mullins began, "your grades have really fallen over the last quarter. What's the problem?"

Ted shrugged his shoulders, "No problem."

"How's your family?"

"Fine."

"Have you thought about going out for the wrestling team?"

"No way," Ted responded too quickly.

"Why not?"

"Cuz those guys are all queers grabbing each other."

Mr. Mullins leaned in toward his desk. "Ted, you're going to have to work at your problems differently. Tell me, have you given any thought to what you'd like to do when you get to high school?"

The bell for lunch period sounded. Mr. Mullins sighed quietly, then stood and walked around the side of his desk. "Okay, Ted," he said. "Okay for now. I'm not going to press you. I want you to give some thought to what we've discussed and to what interests you."

"I don't want to think about that yet," Ted replied.

"Well, maybe you should start. And remember if you're feeling bad about anything, come in and let's talk about it. It's not a good idea for you to bottle up your feelings or to hide your problems."

"Hide?" Ted asked innocently. "I'm not hiding anything."

"Can you believe it," Ted said to Al later that day, "Mullins was tellin' me not to hide stuff. If he only knew!"

"Yeah." Al looked a little hesitantly at Ted. "What are you hiding in your room? Enough to put my dad's liquor cabinet to shame?"

'My parents complained that I was hiding from them.'

Journal Entry: Day 12

I had the greatest hiding places for my stash. I kept a can or two of beer in the toilet tank. But I had to weight them down. They float. I used to hide a six pack in the bottom of my dirty laundry, too, cuz no one in my family would go near that.

Pretty soon, though, getting rid of all those empty cans became a pain. I used to crush them and put them in a garbage bag. Once, my dad found the bag and asked where all the cans came from. I thought I was busted for sure. I told him that I'd collected them for a school recycling project and he bought it! After that close call, I decided to forget about drinking beer at home, too risky. Besides, I could down a whole six pack and not even get buzzed. So I tried vodka again, and it was a whole lot better than when I'd had it the first time, and the bonus: there's no smell.

It was easier hiding marijuana and rolling papers. I could put the papers in my wallet or hide them right in the middle of a pack of loose leaf paper in my room. I hid my pot in one of those ziplock plastic bags and rolled it up in a pair of purple socks that I never wore.

My parents complained that I was hiding from them. Well, they were kinda right. They were always nagging at me about being off by myself or not wanting to be part of family things. But, like, who wants to sit and watch TV with their parents or hang around with them at the mall? Talk about bogus. Whenever I had to do something with family, I tried to get sort of a medium high on just so I could stand it. My parents didn't know I was drinking and using. And they probably wouldn't have found out about it, except for school. That damn school mailed my parents a copy of my report card. When they saw it, man they totally freaked.

It was way uncool!

Ted's dad paced back and forth across the kitchen floor, studying Ted's report card as if it were written in a foreign language. Ted's mom sat quietly at the kitchen table, her hands folded in her lap. Ted lounged across from his mom, doing his best to look cool. He wore an expression that said, "What's the big deal?"

"One F, two D minuses, one D, and a C minus," Ted's dad bellowed, waving the report card. "And you've been absent ten times and tardy nine. What's going on here?" he demanded.

"Chill out, Dad," Ted replied.

"Chill out?"

"I got a bad card. Big deal."

"It is a big deal!" Ted's dad insisted. "You've always been an A-minus, B-plus student, and now you're all but flunking out of school. I think that's a big deal. And I think your mother and I deserve some sort of explanation."

"I already told you that I hated that school," Ted answered. "Everybody's stuck up and I can't concentrate because I hate it so much."

"So what?" his dad interjected. "Do you think I like everything about my work? Do you think I enjoy going in every day or being on time every day? They call it work for a reason, Ted. It's not supposed to be fun."

"All right, all right," said Ted, "I'll work harder next semester."

"Your father and I don't think that will be enough," Ted's mom said softly. "We talked to Mr. Mullins, today. He's agreed to help you set up a study schedule, and he thinks you might find some help by joining one of the support groups at school."

"For what?" Ted snapped.

Ted's mom turned to her son. "Mr. Mullins thinks that you may have a problem with alcohol and other drugs."

An icy chill seemed to push all the air out of Ted's chest. He blinked, then quickly recovered his composure. "Oh, right!" he laughed. "And you believe him?"

"Those beer cans were yours, weren't they?" Ted's dad asked.

"I told you what they were for," Ted said. "If you guys can't trust me then the problem isn't me, it's you."

"Your school never had a recycling project," said Ted's dad.

"See you don't trust me! You had to check up on me."

"No, Ted," his mom replied. "We did trust you, but at the P.T.A. meeting two nights ago, your principal said that he wanted to start a recycling project, beginning next month, because the school had never had one before."

Ted was silent.

"Well?"

"Okay, okay," Ted grimaced. "Just because I lied doesn't mean I'm a drunk."

"What about other drugs, Ted?" his dad asked. "Have you ever used any?"

"No! I swear to God!" said Ted, jumping to his feet. "Why are you guys all over me with this drug stuff just because I had a lousy report card? I never drank anything stronger than beer, okay? And I never touched any other drugs!"

Ted looked at his seated parents. Neither spoke. Slowly, his mom unfolded her hands. There, in her lap, rested an empty half-pint bottle of vodka and a rolled up pair of purple socks.

Ted closed his eyes. "If I'm on trial here, I demand a lawyer." He could only think of one thing. He needed a drink or a joint.

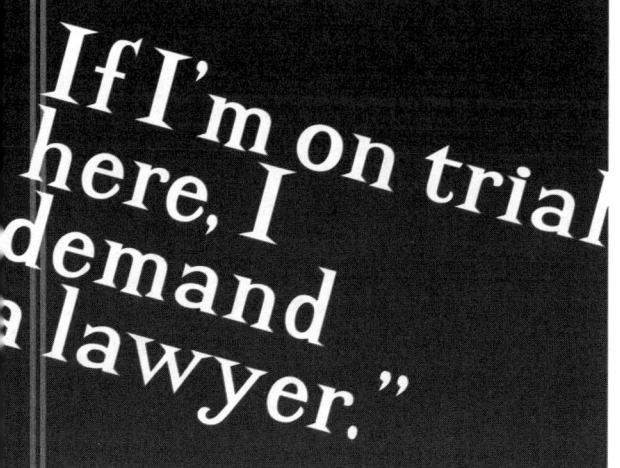

If I'm on trial here, I demand a lawyer.

Journal Entry: Day 14

Things are lookin' up in this place.

At least we get to do something besides listen to counselors and group work. Last night I got to help fix supper. We made chili. Everyone said it was grubbin'. I bet Al would have liked it. But maybe not.

The front of Al's house was dark. But Ted could see a shaft of light coming from the kitchen window in the rear. He ran around the side of the house and pounded on the back door.

"Open up, Al," he shouted. "Come on, man, hustle!"

Al peered through the curtained window. When he saw his friend, he opened the door, but left the safety chain hooked.

"Hey, dude, how ya doin'? What's the problem? You look wasted."

"The problem is I'm not wasted. I need a drink or a hit, man."

"Whoa! Slow down, guy." Al said. "Maybe you should head for home, you know? You don't look so good."

"I don't look so good? If you

don't open this damn door in ten seconds, you ain't gonna look so good," Ted threatened.

"Aw, dude, there ain't no booze in here, and I'm not holdin' anything either. I told you that last week. I'm off all that stuff. You better go home, okay?"

With a quick rush, Ted slammed his shoulder into the door. There was an angry ripping sound as the chain popped and tore away a large section of the door molding. The door swung open violently, knocking Al across the room and onto the floor.

"Owwww," Al whimpered and clutched at his left arm. "What the hell, dude! I think you busted my arm." He tried to stand, but his legs failed him, so he cried out, "Get the hell out of here!"

Ted was rapidly opening the kitchen cupboards one after another and pulling out cups, plates, glasses, and canned goods, and strewing them across the kitchen. "Where is it, Al? Don't B.S. me, man. I know you got somethin' stashed."

"Geez!" Al winced and ducked an airborne can of chili. "I told you. I quit that crap. It was messin' me up. And, dude, it's sure screwin' you. Get the hell out of here, or I'm gonna call the cops. I mean it!"

Ted whirled around and looked dangerously at Al. "Shut up! Shut up, you little freak, and tell me where the stuff is!"

Al's eyes had gone wide, and his face had turned a sickly shade of gray. Al wasn't looking at Ted, but at Ted's right hand. There was something so odd about Al's look that it took Ted a moment to figure out what it was. It wasn't anger that Ted saw in his friend. It was fear.

Ted glanced down at his right hand. It was a large hand, knuckles whitened with tension, fingers clenched around the handle of a large and menacing kitchen knife—pointed right at Al.

Ted began to shake. His arms went limp. The knife clattered to the floor. Ted slid to the floor himself and bent his head to his knees, making his body into a tight and trembling ball. Al lay in one corner of the kitchen, still clutching his broken arm. Ted lay in the other, quietly sobbing.

That's how Ted's dad found them.

"I told you. I quit that crap, It was messin' me up."

Journal Entry: Day 20

Damn! I must've broken the lead on this pencil about ten times tryin' to get started on this thing today. I gotta get movin' on this. Tomorrow is the start of family week, and I'm pretty nervous about my parents comin' here and all. I'm working up a sweat like it was summer, and it's barely spring.

I know they'll ask me why, why I did it, why I drank and used. I don't think they'll understand. See, I did it because I needed it! Well, maybe not at first. At first, I did it because I didn't like feeling the way I did. I was tired of hurting. Booze helped. Dope helped. But after a while, nothing helped much. I wasn't turnin' on to drugs any more. They were turnin' on me. But I didn't stop. I couldn't. I just kept doing it.

I kept doing it because I wanted to feel normal—just make it through the day. Pretty soon, I didn't care. It wasn't so much that I did it cuz I didn't want to feel bad. Hell, I did it cuz I didn't want to feel anything. Period.

"Yo, journaling period's over," announced a staff member who'd poked his head into Ted's room. "Shake it, Ted. Your family's here."

Ted stood up, closed his journal, and headed out into the hallway. He rounded the corner and spotted his mom and dad. Their backs were to him, and they were talking to someone. As Ted drew closer, his parents turned and smiled, but their eyes seemed sad. Then Ted saw that the person his parents were talking to was someone whose left arm sported a bright purple cast from shoulder to thumb. It was Al. He cracked a crooked smile, raised his arm in a royal purple salute, and said, "Hey, dude, how you doin'?"

Journal Entry: Day 21

I felt good today. One day at a time.

Write your first reactions to the story. Don't concentrate on grammar or style. Just try to get to the truth.

What do you think the title means? Is it serious or sarcastic?

At the story's end, Ted seems to be recovering from his alcohol and other drug use. What might help or hinder him in trying to stay clean?

Why do you think Al says "It's Miller Time"? Think of all the alcohol ads you see every day. Which ones stay with you? Why?

Have you ever been able to hurt and help a friend the way Al did?

Write about someone who had a serious problem like alcohol or other drug use in his or her family. What struck you about this problem?

Before reading about the MADD campaign and Peg McCormick, choose sides and debate whether states have the right to stop cars for sobriety checks.

DATELINE: WASHINGTON, D.C. MOTHERS AGAINST DRUNK DRIVING (MADD) LAUNCHED A "SAFE HOLIDAY" CAMPAIGN OF SOBRIETY CHECKS TO CURB ALCOHOL-RELATED TRAFFIC DEATHS AND INJURIES OVER THE 4TH OF JULY WEEKEND— THE DEADLIEST WEEKEND ON THE NATION'S HIGHWAYS....

CONSIDER PEG MCCORMICK'S STORY

She was one of the speakers on the front lawn of the Capitol Building in Washington in 1992.

Six years before standing in front of the television cameras that day of the MADD campaign launch, Peg McCormick kissed her two daughters, Cathy 19 and Sara 15, as they left to watch the fireworks on the Fourth of July. When they called about 11:30 p.m. to say they were on their way home, Peg and her husband Terry, began the wait they had no idea would end in such tragedy. After an hour went by and the girls hadn't returned from a 30-minute ride by car, Peg was telephoning the girls' friends who assured them that their daughters left when they said they had. Another hour and still no word. When the police finally arrived, Terry admitted the terrible truth to Peg that he had known with certainty that they were dead 20 minutes after they phoned.

At the hospital, they had to wage a quiet battle. Hospital personnel told them that only Terry would be allowed to identify the girls in the morgue. Peg knew that she had to see and touch her daughters one more time. "Where is it written," she asked, "that only fathers must identify the broken bodies of their children?" Before the sheet was even lifted, Peg recognized Cathy's hand. The girls had each let their grandmother give them manicures that day—just because it always made the elderly woman so happy.

"I beg every American this Fourth of July and every day and night: please don't drink and drive," Peg said. "When a drunk driver takes away a child, it's not an 'accident,' it's murder, pure and simple."

Peg McCormick's words make up a personal story. People who know Peg say that her story has made them much more conscious about their own drinking-and-driving behavior. Do you know any real stories of alcohol-related deaths? Why do real stories have much more impact on your actions than statistics or news reports do?

MUSIC

TROUBLE WITH THE SWEET STUFF

"I've got trouble with the sweet stuff
and I'm never ever never gonna shake it/
Trouble with the sweet stuff/
Don't wanna give it up
shake it
got to give it up
don't wanna give it up
never never never
gonna shake it
can't give it up."

© 1990 Billy Idol, BoneIdol Music/ Chrysalis Music (ASCAP)/
Swindle Music (ASCAP)/ Texas Twang Tunes (ASCAP)

THE DAYS OF WINE AND ROSES

"Laugh and run away like a child at play
through the meadowland toward a closing
door,
a door marked nevermore that wasn't
there before.
The lonely night discloses just a passing
breeze,
filled with memories of the golden smile
that introduced me to the days of wine
and roses and you."

© 1962 Johnny Mercer (lyrics) Henry Mancini (music)
M. Witmark & Sons

What's the song about when one track carries "got to give it up" and the simultaneous track says "can't give it up"? What do you think: do we all have conflicts like this? Or, do drugs make this kind of conflict really different?

Check out the record from the library, or rent the video, of "The Days of Wine and Roses." Why is it considered a classic expression of what alcohol abuse can do to lives? Do you think the song captures the excitement and the downfall of alcohol?

America's first drug crisis was in the 1920s. Before then, films such as *The Mystery of the Leaping Fish* with Douglas Fairbanks could get away with spoofing drug smuggling. But drug addiction and smuggling became real in the 1920s and have been treated moralistically ever since. Escaping drug and alcohol addiction are often movie themes. Have you seen any of these video classics?

What does a film on drug use do that a novel or essay may not be able to do?

OPIUM DENS

1919 Broken Blossoms
1971 McCabe and Mrs. Miller
1984 Once Upon A Time in America

HEROIN WITHDRAWAL

1923 Human Wreckage
1955 The Man With the Golden Arm
1975 French Connection II

MARIJUANA USE

1936 Reefer Madness
1987 Less Than Zero

PRO-DRUG FILMS

1967 The Trip
1968 Psych-Out
1969 Easy Rider

THE GRIM SIDE

1981 Prince of the City
1972 Ciao! Manhattan
1988 Clean and Sober
1989 Drugstore Cowboy
1990 Goodfellas

Just one tittle,
Just one jot,
Just one bottle,
That's a lot.
—Anonymous

I'M YOUR NEW GOD
BY SIR MIXALOT (MACK DADDY)

The rapster tells several stories of the power cocaine has over people.

Kneel to me/ smoke me/ breathe me
I'm your new god
you can call me cocaine.

I try to get a young kid
but he just said no
because of some sports hero
so I entered the hero's house
in the form of a line
and let him snort one time.
Now he's dead cuz my dose was pure:
got it too quick for the cure,
so the headlines read:
dope made another hit
dead on the first sniff...

©West Mix Records, 1992

DRUGS
KEVIN, AGE 11

Dope is something
that can knock you out.
Dope is something
that can kill you.
It just takes you in,
and kind of sends you
out and out.

From *Somebody Real / Voices of City Children*
American Faculty Press, New Jersey, 1972

SUMMER WORDS
OF A SISTUH ADDICT
BY SONIA SANCHEZ

the first day i shot dope
was on a sunday.
        I had just come
home from church
        got mad at my motha
cuz she got mad at me.   u dig?
        went out. shot up
behind a feelen gainst her.
        it felt good.
gooder than dooing it. yeah.
        it was nice.
i did it. "uh-huh." i did it.   "uh-huh."
i want to do it again...

From *We a BaddDDD People*,
by Sonia Sanchez Knight Broadside Press, 1970

HUMOR

Drug and alcohol abuse are serious problems needing serious solutions. Sometimes, though, laughing at a problem is one good way of facing it.

"You grow up the day you have your first real laugh— at yourself."
—Ethel Barrymore

Perhaps the reason we joke about alcoholics is the same reason we whistle while walking through a cemetery at night.
—Anonymous

Too much of anything is bad, but too much of good whiskey is barely enough.
—Mark Twain

Drink always rubbed him the right way.
—Ogden Nash

It is said that these two jokes promote drinking. What do you think?

_____

_____

_____

_____

_____

Is it often that drinking or drug use gets started from feeling "misunderstood" as described in Sonia Sanchez's poem?

_____

_____

_____

_____

LIT-BITS

Authors such as Faulkner, Hemingway, Steinbeck, Lewis, or O'Neill wrote while under the influence. Other authors simply comment on alcohol and other drugs.

OTHELLO
A TRAGEDY BY WILLIAM SHAKESPEARE

Iago, Othello's lieutenant, suggests that Othello's wife Desdemona has been unfaithful to him. The culprit is Cassio, Iago says, and sets Cassio up for the drama by getting him drunk. He says to his cohort, "We must get him drunk. If he drinks he is ruined." It works: Cassio gets drunk, behaves badly and that sets the image in Othello's eyes. Cassio apologizes to Othello: "I have very poor and unhappy brains for drinking; I could wish courtesy would invent some other custom of entertainment."

Do you know of a situation where someone coerced another into drinking and something bad happened?

A jug of wine, a loaf of bread and thou. **Omar Khayyam** is famous for this romantic line of verse. He also saw in wine a refuge from the hopelessness of ever knowing the ultimate mystery:

Yesterday This Day's Madness did prepare;
To-morrow's Silence, Triumph, or Despair:
Drink! for you know not whence you came, nor why:
Drink! for you know not why you go, nor where.

Why do you think "big" questions about life make some people turn to drink or other drugs for answers?

"If we pour ourselves immense draughts, it will be no time before both our bodies and our minds reel."
— Socrates

Junior Addict
by Langston Hughes

The little boy
who sticks a needle in his arm
and seeks an out in other worldly
dreams,

cannot know, of course,
(and has no way to understand)
a sunrise that he cannot see
beginning in some other land—
and destined sure to flood . . .
the very room in which today the air
is heavy with the drug
of his despair.
      (Yet little can
      tomorrow's sunshine give
      to one who will not live.)
Quick, sunrise, come!
Sunrise out of Africa,
Quick, come!
Sunrise, please come!
Come! Come!

from *The Panther and the Lash*
Alfred A. Knopf, New York, 1967

Writers, filmmakers, poets–all speak about alcohol in both harsh and glowing terms. Talk about how these two sides of alcohol are expressed. Does paradox fit into this debate?

What does a sense of the future do for you? Why should having something to look forward to influence our drug use?

"One of the disadvantages of wine is that it makes a man mistake words for thoughts."
—Dr. Samuel Johnson

"Ah, bottle, my friend, why do you empty yourself?"
—Moliére

"Wine makes a man better pleased with himself; I do not say that it makes him more pleasing to others."
—Dr. Samuel Johnson

First the man takes a drink
Then the drink takes a drink
Then the drink takes the man.
—Japanese proverb

TELEVISION

On *The Cosby Show,* daughter Vanessa comes home after a party, and her parents find her with her head in her waste-basket moaning about how sick she feels from her drunken evening.

The Huxtable family all get in on the act of tricking Vanessa and all ends happily with Vanessa promising never to drink again.

Is getting drunk funny? What if the drug chosen was cocaine or acid? How would a TV sitcom deal with it? Do you think getting sick from a hangover teaches a good lesson? How should drugs be shown on TV?

YOU THOUGHT IT COULDN'T HAPPEN TO YOU

Lives are affected by drugs only in the movies, you might tell yourself—"It'll never happen to me." Listen to these true stories.

PETER'S STORY

from "We Have a Problem," James Marks, Parents, 1989

The worst came one evening when Tom (Peter's dad) confronted Peter. 'Did you take some money from my desk?' he demanded. I intervened angrily and said, 'Tom, you know he wouldn't! You must have spent it yourself or mis-placed it. It happens to me all the time.'

Tom backed off and apologized to Peter…. The next day I bought the new U2 tape and left it on Peter's bed. I had to let him know that one of his parents loved and trusted him 100 percent.

When Peter and Amy (his favorite aunt who had dealt with her own drug problem) came back from a walk one night, Amy said to his parents, "You need to know what's going on with your son. And I want Peter to tell you." Peter looked at her with pure hatred. Then, in a joking tone, he said, "She thinks I'm a drug addict."

"Yes," Amy said calm-ly. "Peter told me that he's been smoking pot since the first week of school, and now he's using cocaine. Haven't you noticed your money missing? Tell them, Peter —how your mom bought you a tape, but you still took money from her wallet that same night."

Do you think Peter's parents are part of the problem? Did his aunt do the right thing in your opinion?

DAVID'S STORY

from "The Trouble with David,"
Readers Digest/Plain Dealer Magazine
Cleveland, Ohio, May 3, 1987

"The morning of the intervention our team assembled to confront David. The psychologist brought along two bright young people who had been recent subjects of intervention. They would identify with David and assure him about the treatment center."

"The psychologist planned the seating in our living room, with a place for David farthest from the door. But when he entered the room and saw the group, he slid through a side door to the garage and fled down the driveway. I raced after him and persuaded him to return..."

"'David,' I began, 'over the past two years you have fallen apart before our eyes. You have deteriorated intellectually, socially, morally and maybe even physically...You can have alcohol or you can have everything else beautiful in the world, but you can't have both.'"

Why do you suppose David came back with his mother? Do you think the choice she gave him was a genuine one?

HAVE YOU READ?

THE BOY WHO DRANK TOO MUCH

Shep Greene, Dell Publishing, 1979

Buff grew up living with his alcoholic and abusive father. To cope with his life, he begins drinking. Hockey and a couple true friends save him and he gets the chance to begin again.

I kept rolling thoughts about Buff over and over in my mind. I didn't know how to help him. I couldn't help him the way he helped me... His problem was much more complicated. And frankly, I didn't want to help him any more...

"Come on," Julie shouted at me. "I've found Buff..." We raced out of the room, down the corridor... By the time we got to the tennis courts, four seventh-graders in gym shorts had found Buff, too. They were staring at him and laughing.

"He just peed in his pants," one of them said...

"What's wrong with him?" one kid asked.

"He's sick," I said... "He's got mono..."

They left and I tried to get Buff to shape up. He groaned and his head rolled around like it was about to fall off. But I couldn't make him snap out of it.

"He's drunk, isn't he?" Julie asked.

Respond to this scene. To friends getting tired of helping but then helping anyway. To kids laughing. To friends covering for each other.

THIS TIME IN AMERICA

A BRIEF HISTORY OF DRUGS IN AMERICA

In the thousand years before drugs were produced artificially, they were available only in their natural forms. People chewed coca leaves or poppy plants, or dropped them in alcohol to dissolve them and extract the cocaine and morphine.

In the 1800s, the scientific achievement of organic chemistry altered the form of drugs.

Morphine was isolated by 1810, cocaine by 1860.

The Bayer Company introduced heroin as a cough syrup in 1898; the next year they introduced aspirin.

In 1906, the Federal Food and Drug Act required accurate labeling of drugs but did not restrict use.

Benjamin Franklin took opium in alcohol extract for pain relief.

In the 1920s, Eugene O'Neill's play, *A Long Day's Journey Into Night,* showed a family devastated by a mother's drug addiction caused by a careless physician's prescriptions.

Look up the Harrison Act and talk about the impact it made on drugs at that time. Is it still influential in dealing with drug abuse today?

In 1887, famous neurologist, William Hammond, assured people that cocaine was no more habit-forming than coffee or tea.

In the late 1880s, Coca-Cola was introduced as a drink lacking the dangers of alcohol but offering the advantages of coca.

In 1900, cocaine was removed from Coca-Cola because it was found to be harmful.

In the early 1900s, Parke-Davis Pharmaceuticals supplied 15 different forms of cocaine and announced that the drug "makes the coward brave, the silent eloquent...."

In 1914, William Howard Taft signed the Harrison Act, which required a strict accounting of opium and coca and derivatives.

In 1900, cocaine was seen as a grand drug; in the last decade of the 1900s it is seen as a most dangerous drug.

THE RISE AND FALL OF DRUG POPULARITY

As a group, do some research on various drugs, their histories, use and abuse, and legal battles. Then debate the legalization issues; take one side and then reverse your position and debate the other side.

In the 1960s and 1970s mainstream society increased its use of opiates and cocaine because the physiological and emotional effects were considered to be enjoyable.

In the 1960s and 1970s, many people believed that drugs enhanced potential and that bad experiences with drugs were the exception.

In recent times, it has become more common for people to believe that drugs reduce human achievement, and more emphasis is being placed on healthy food and exercise.

Marijuana

In 1920, Mexican immigrants brought the cannabis plant to the U.S. The Marijuana Tax Act of 1937 prohibited its use. Not until the 1960s did marijuana use became widespread. The demand for it grew until 1978. In 1980, 53 percent of the population favored legalization. By 1986, only 27 percent supported it. In 1990, popular vote reversed possession and use of marijuana to a crime with strict penalties.

Alcoholism, no respecter of the famous, aided the decline of these famous people.

EDGAR ALLAN POE

1809-49, American short story writer, poet, father of the modern detective story.

A slight person, Poe couldn't take even one drink without it greatly affecting him. Two drinks were disastrous, and more reduced him to a blubbering idiot. He died at 40 after a drinking bout.

MODEST MOUSSORGSKY

1839-81, Russian composer.

Moussorgsky was famous for *A Night on Bald Mountain, Pictures at an Exhibition*, and his opera *Boris Godunov*.

His career declined while he was in his early thirties due to his chronic alcoholism, and his death at 42 was caused by alcoholic epilepsy.

JIMI HENDRIX

1942-1970

Credited with reinventing the way electric guitar is played, Jimi Hendrix enjoyed a brilliant but tragically short career. His albums are still considered revolutionary approaches to rock music.

Hendrix died at 27 from a drug overdose, leaving the music world to wonder what new musical ground Hendrix might have broken had he not died so young.

SOME OTHER ALCOHOLICS FROM HISTORY'S ANNALS

Douglas Fairbanks, actor

King Edward VIII of England, Duke of Windsor

Isadora Duncan, dancer

Eugene V. Debs, presidential candidate

Edna St. Vincent Millay, poet

Rube Waddell, baseball pitcher

Jim Thorpe, football and baseball player, track star

Grover Cleveland Alexander, baseball pitcher

Tommy Armour, golfer

Some people fall hard and prematurely into decline because of their abuse of alcohol. Some people continue to thrive and produce all the while they are abusing alcohol. What's your opinion? Is alcohol the problem? If people are able to survive AND keep drinking, does that make alcohol abuse okay?